FLORETTE

by Anna Walker

Clarion Books

Houghton Mifflin Harcourt
Boston   New York

For Wendy Anne, with love

Clarion Books
3 Park Avenue
New York, New York 10016

Clarion Books is an imprint of
Houghton Mifflin Harcourt Publishing Company.

www.hmhco.com

The illustrations in this book were done in watercolor.
The text was set in 14 pt. Letterpress Text.

Library of Congress Cataloging-in-Publication Data is available.
ISBN 978-0-544-87683-5

Manufactured in China
SCP 10 9 8 7 6 5 4 3 2 1
4500682631

When Mae's family moved to the city,
Mae wanted to bring her garden with her.

Her mother said she could
make a new garden.
But there was no room among
the crowded buildings
for apple trees and daffodils.

Instead of winding paths and leafy hiding spots,
all Mae found was a cranky cat.

And boxes.
Lots of boxes.

Mae missed playing with her friends,
listening to the birds in the apple trees,
and gathering things for her treasure jar.

She longed to chase butterflies
in the wavy grass.
She drew her own butterflies...

but the rain washed them away.

She set up a picnic . . .

but the apple tree fell over,
and the daisies went missing.

Mae was tired of those boxes.

Down below, people moved like ants
winding through the streets.
Beyond them, Mae spied an open space.
A space with trees and a swing.
When Mae's mother was ready to go out,
Mae ran downstairs
and led the way
on a new path.

She turned the corner
and walked over a bridge . . .

between the buildings . . .

and under lampposts
until she came to a park.

A park filled
with tiny stones

and empty chairs.

Mae drew a daisy in the pebbles.

She listened to the hum of the city
and the rustle
of a tiny bird.

An apple-tree bird!

The bird took flight, and Mae quickly followed,
only to see it disappear . . .

into a leafy forest.

But the forest was closed.

Mae waited. And waited. The bird did not come out.

Mae stared at the entrance for a very long time.

FLORETTE

Then she noticed a small green sprout
peeking through a gap . . .

a piece of forest.

Mae walked back around the corner.
She hopped over tiny stones

and passed empty chairs.

She weaved through the streets,
under lampposts

and back over the bridge.

At home, Mae held her new
treasure up to the light.

On the windowsill was her jar.

A small jar

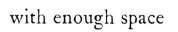

with enough space

for a plant to grow...

in Mae's garden.